First published in 2010
by Wayland

Text copyright © Jillian Powell
Illustration copyright © Amanda Gulliver

Wayland
338 Euston Road
London NW1 3BH

Wayland Australia
Level 17/207 Kent Street
Sydney, NSW 2000

Series Editor: Louise John
Editor: Katie Powell
Cover design: Paul Cherrill
Design: D.R.ink
Consultant: Shirley Bickler

A CIP catalogue record for this book is available from the British Library.

ISBN 9780750260664

Printed in China

Wayland is a division of Hachette Children's Books,
an Hachette UK Company

www.hachette.co.uk

Fun Run

Written by Jillian Powell
Illustrated by Amanda Gulliver

WAYLAND

We ran past
the start line.

We ran past a tomato.

START

We ran past a chicken.

We ran past a rabbit.

We ran past a clown.

We ran past a horse.

We ran past a snowman.

We ran past
a caterpillar.

We ran past
the finish line.
Hurray!

Guiding a First Read of
Fun Run

It is important to talk through the book with the child before they read it alone. This prepares them for the way the story unfolds, and allows them to enjoy the pictures as you both talk naturally, using the language they will later encounter when reading. Read them the brief overview, and then follow the suggestions below:

1. Talking through the book
The title of this book is 'Fun Run'. In this book all the children are in fancy dress. The two children in the big funny hats tell us how they ran past all the others runners.

Let's read the title: **Fun Run**
Look at the pictures on page 4.
The children are at the start line.
They said, "We ran past the start line."
Now turn to page 6. Here they said,
"We ran past a tomato."

Continue through the book, guiding the discussion to fit the text as the child looks at the illustrations.

Look on page 20. It's the finish line,
so what did they say?
"We ran past the finish line."
And did they win the race?
Yes. Hurray!

2. A first reading of the book

Ask the child to read the book independently, pointing carefully under each word (tracking), while thinking about the story. Praise attempts by the child to correct themselves, and prompt them to use their letter knowledge, the punctuation and check the meaning, for example:

You said, 'the rabbit' and then you changed it yourself to 'a rabbit'. That's what good readers do.

Your pointing was lovely and you looked very carefully. Now try reading it again and make the story sound exciting.

3. Follow-up activities

The high frequency words in this title are:

a   the   we

- Select a new high frequency word, and ask the child to find it throughout the book. Discuss the shape of the letters and the letter sounds.
- To memorise the word, ask the child to write it in the air, then write it repeatedly on a whiteboard or on paper, leaving a space between each attempt.

4. Encourage

- Reading the book again – with expression.
- Drawing a picture based on the story.
- Writing one or two sentences using the practised words.

START READING is a series of highly enjoyable books for beginner readers. **The books have been carefully graded to match the Book Bands widely used in schools.** This enables readers to be sure they choose books that match their own reading ability.

Look out for the Band colour on the book in our Start Reading logo.

The Bands are:

	Pink Band 1A & 1B
	Red Band 2
	Yellow Band 3
	Blue Band 4
	Green Band 5
	Orange Band 6
	Turquoise Band 7
	Purple Band 8
	Gold Band 9

START READING books can be read independently or shared with an adult. They promote the enjoyment of reading through satisfying stories supported by fun illustrations.

Jillian Powell started writing stories when she was four years old. She has written many books for children, including stories about cats, dogs, scarecrows and ghosts. Jillian loves being outdoors, just like the children in Get Up and Go!

Amanda Gulliver always enjoyed art at school and went on to study Graphics and Illustration at College in Cornwall. Amanda now lives just a ten minute walk from the sea, where she can be found on the beach building sandcastles and collecting sea shells with her husband and two daughters.